A BOY WANTS A DINOSAUR

ISBN 0-590-46142-7

Text copyright © 1990 by Hiawyn Oram.
Illustrations copyright © 1990 by Satoshi Kitamura.
All rights reserved. Published by Scholastic Inc.,
730 Broadway, New York, NY 10003, by arrangement with
Farrar Straus & Giroux.
First published in Great Britain by Andersen Press, Ltd., 1990.

12 11 10 9 8 7 6 5 4 3   3 4 5 6 7/9

Printed in the U.S.A.   09
First Scholastic printing, December 1992

A BOY WANTS A DINOSAUR

HIAWYN ORAM
SATOSHI KITAMURA

SCHOLASTIC INC.
New York Toronto London
Auckland Sydney

Ben had a dog.
Alice had two snails.
Alex wanted a dinosaur.

He lay on his bed and cried.
"But I want a dinosaur."
He sobbed until his grandfather put down his saxophone, put on his hat and coat, and said, "A boy wants a dinosaur this much, a boy should have a dinosaur . . ."

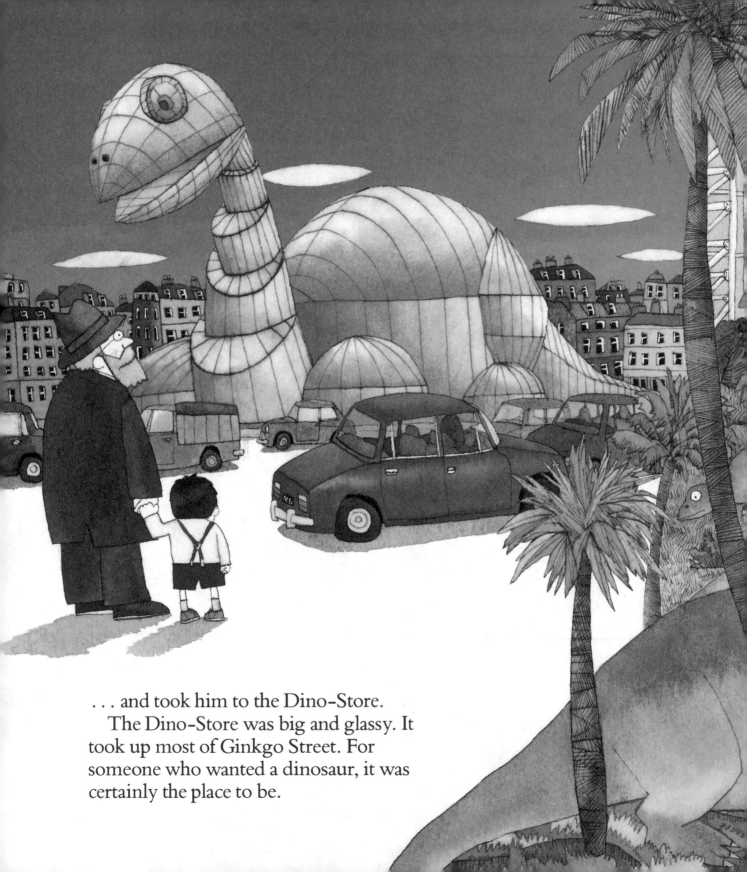

. . . and took him to the Dino-Store.
    The Dino-Store was big and glassy. It took up most of Ginkgo Street. For someone who wanted a dinosaur, it was certainly the place to be.

On the first floor were the grown dinosaurs. On the second floor were the young dinosaurs. In the basement, the baby Hadrosaurus splashed in the Hadrosaurium.

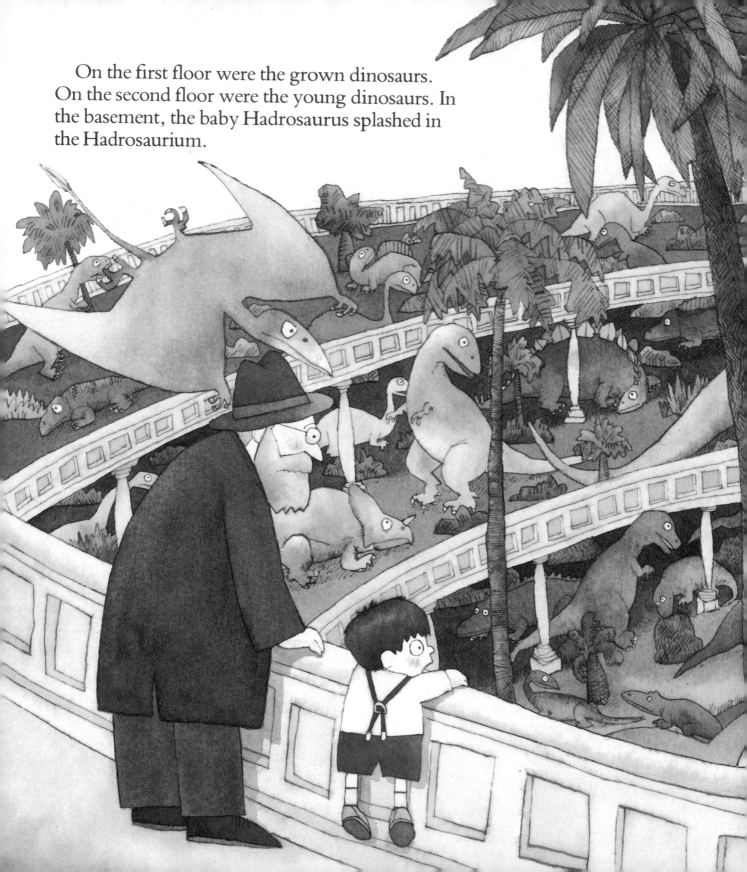

On the top floor, the Pterosaurs soared in the Pterosaviary, and on the third floor there was everything you could ever need for a dinosaur.

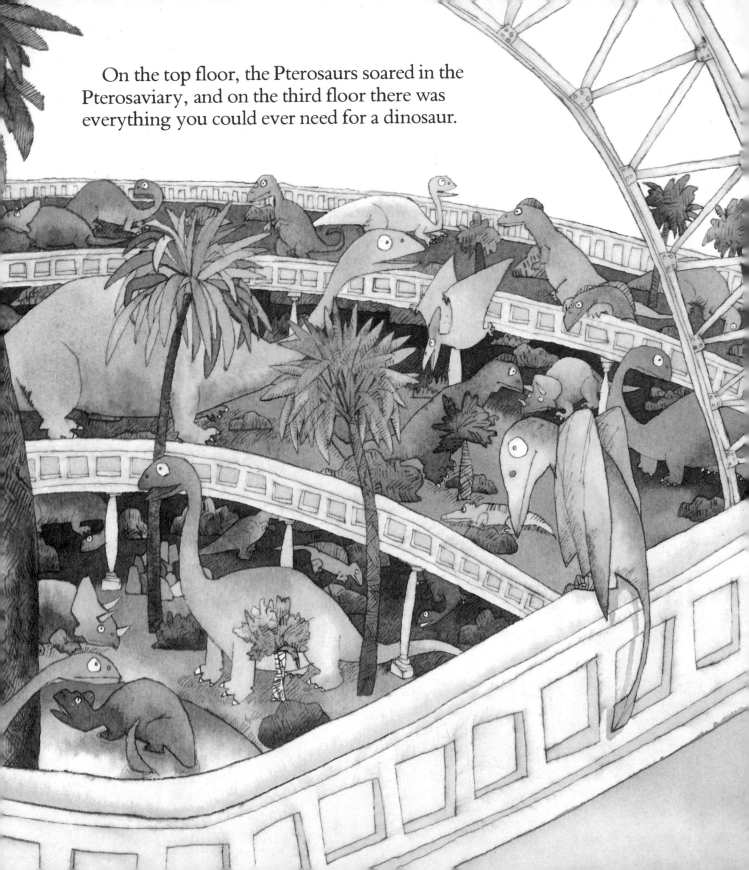

First, Alex thought he wanted a Triceratops. Then he thought he wanted a Fabrosaur. Then, just as he had almost decided on a Diplodocus, he saw the Massospondylus and the Massospondylus saw him

and came over and rolled on its back and rolled its eyes and
licked Alex's hand.

"I'll call him Fred," said Alex.

"But she's a girl," said his grandfather, reading the sign.
"A girl who eats anything — meat and plants!"

"Then I'll call her The One Who Eats Everything, but Fred
for short," said Alex, and they ordered what she would need,
put on her collar and lead, and set off for home.

When they got home, Alex could not wait to see Fred eat . . . two bags of fossils soaked in all the milk in the fridge, one drum of dried club-moss tree, three sacks of pine needles, the washing, the neighbor's zucchini, and a bite out of the next-door-but-one's cat.

"Alex!" said his mother. "This is really too much!"

But Alex would not listen. "Not for a dinosaur," he said. "For a dinosaur it is only a snack . . ."

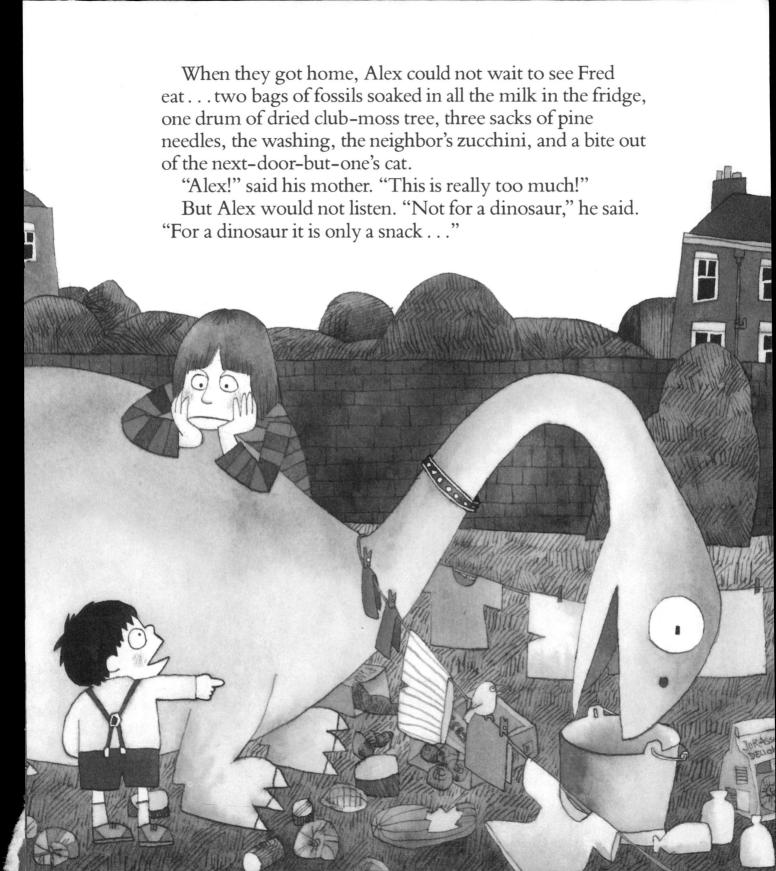

And he dashed upstairs, ran a steaming–hot bath, added some Instant Marsh Powder, and put Fred in for a good long soak.

"Alex," called his father, coming in from work, "a marsh in the house is quite unhealthy!"

"Not for a dinosaur," Alex replied crossly. "For a dinosaur it is perfectly natural . . ."

And he sneaked Fred into his room and sang to her in
Massospondylus until he fell asleep, and did not notice
that she couldn't settle and chewed everything she
could find in the dark to comfort her.

When Alex's mother came in in the morning, she threw her hands in the air and sat on the bed stump and wailed and cried.

"But it's terrible," she wailed. "Monstrous and prehistoric!"

"Not for a dinosaur," Alex explained as patiently as he could. "For a dinosaur it's much more like home . . ."

And he dressed and put on Fred's collar
and lead and set off for school. On the way,
Fred spotted a truck turning a corner, and
bounded into the road and lashed out.

The truck driver was furious. "Do you mind!" he yelled. "This is my company's best truck!"

"Not to my dinosaur," Alex yelled back, losing his temper. "To my dinosaur it's probably a Tyrannosaurus Rex!"

And he dragged Fred away and into school. Alex's friends were very excited about having a dinosaur in Pets' Corner, but Miss Jenkins was not so sure.

"A classroom is a place for sitting still, for listening and learning with no distractions," she said.

"Not for my dinosaur," said Alex. "This classroom is making her feel very, very sick."

And he ran and got his grandfather and they took Fred to the vet. The vet looked at Fred's tongue and listened to her heart and shone a light into her eyes. He asked about the fight with the truck and X-rayed her for broken bones.

"Well?" asked Alex. "What is it? What's the matter with her?"

"Nothing that a nice long walk in the country won't cure," said the vet.

And there amid the fields of sheep and barns of hay Fred perked up. She gamboled and lolloped, lumbered and strode, and would not stop until they reached the other side of a thick pine forest.

Running after her, Alex saw why. Stretching all around them was a crusty old swamp edged by giant club-moss trees. Fred reared up and ran for it.

"Now, Fred!" yelled Alex. "This is going too far!"

"NOT FOR A DINOSAUR!" shouted Alex's grandfather, and with a bubbling-under shout . . .

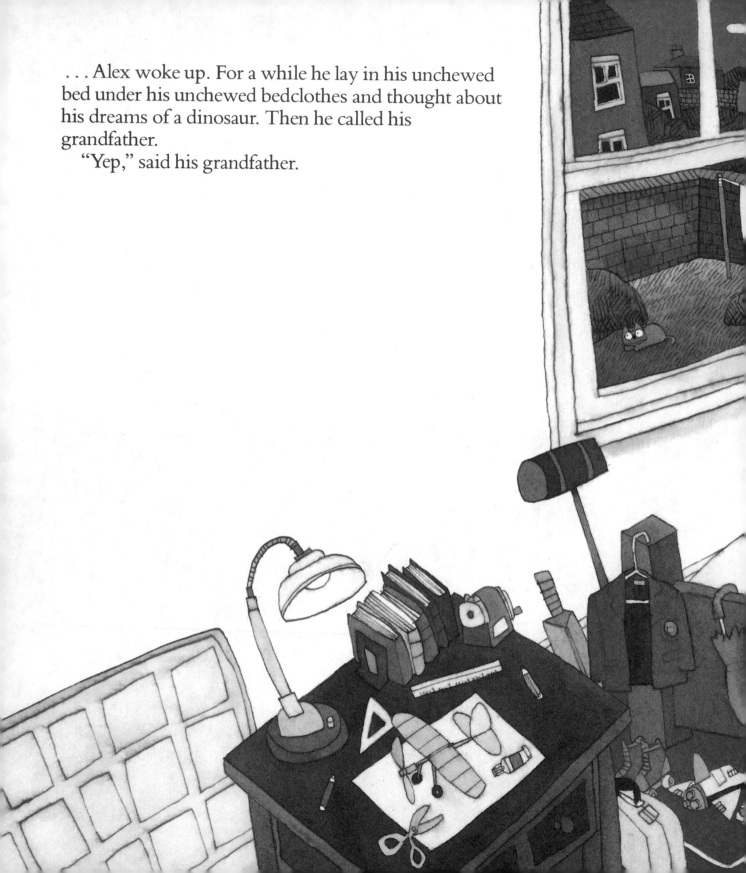

. . . Alex woke up. For a while he lay in his unchewed bed under his unchewed bedclothes and thought about his dreams of a dinosaur. Then he called his grandfather.

"Yep," said his grandfather.

"When we get a pet, I think we should get . . ."
"A rabbit?" said his grandfather.
"Exactly," said Alex. "And we won't call her
Fred either."